My First Ph

I Like to Look

by Janelle Cherrington
Illustrated by Vincent Andriani

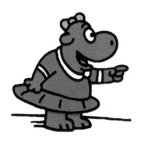

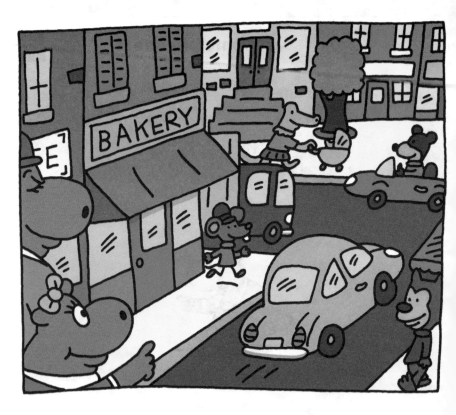

I like to look.

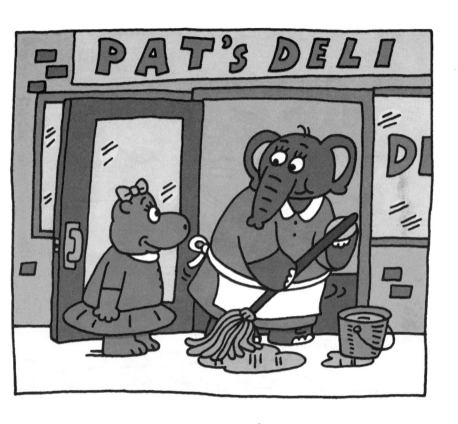

I see Pat and a mop.

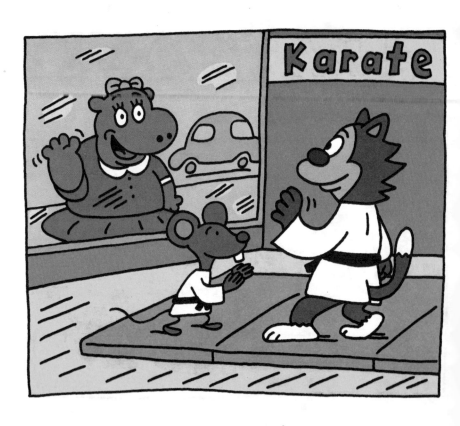

I see Dan on the mat.

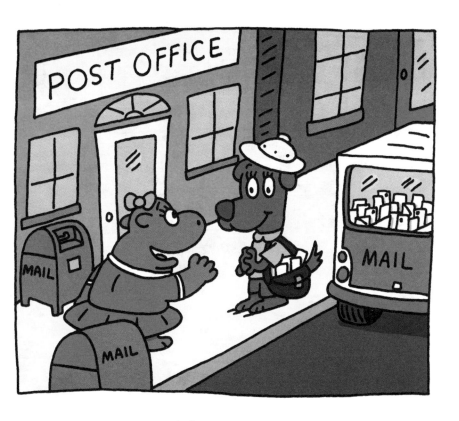

I like Pam.

5

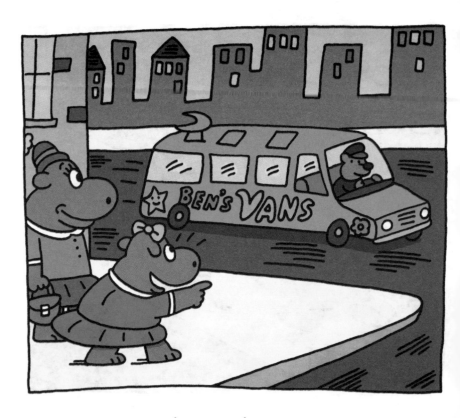

Look at the van!

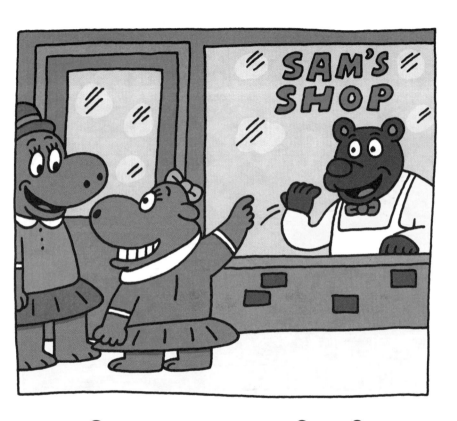

Can we go see Sam?

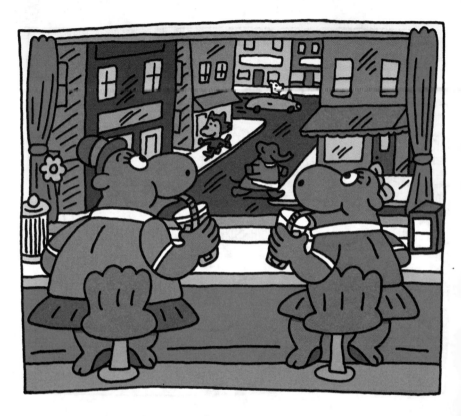

What do you see?